KT-491-305

50

LOVE

For Sheniz and Noah ~ C.F.

For Nia ~ B.C.

SIMON AND SCHUSTER
This paperback edition first published in Great Britain in 2016
by Simon and Schuster UK Ltd
1st Floor, 222 Gray's Inn Road, London WC1X 8HB
A CBS COMPANY

Text copyright © 2015 Claire Freedman
Illustrations copyright © 2015 Ben Cort

The right of Claire Freedman and Ben Cort to be identified as the author and illustrator of this work has been asserted by them in accordance with the Copyright, Designs and Patents Act, 1988

All rights reserved, including the right of reproduction in whole or in part in any form

A CIP catalogue record for this book is available from the British Library upon request

ISBN: 978-1-4711-2095-4 (PB)
ISBN: 978-1-4711-2096-1 (eBook)

Printed in China
3 5 7 9 10 8 6 4 2

Aliens Love Dinopants

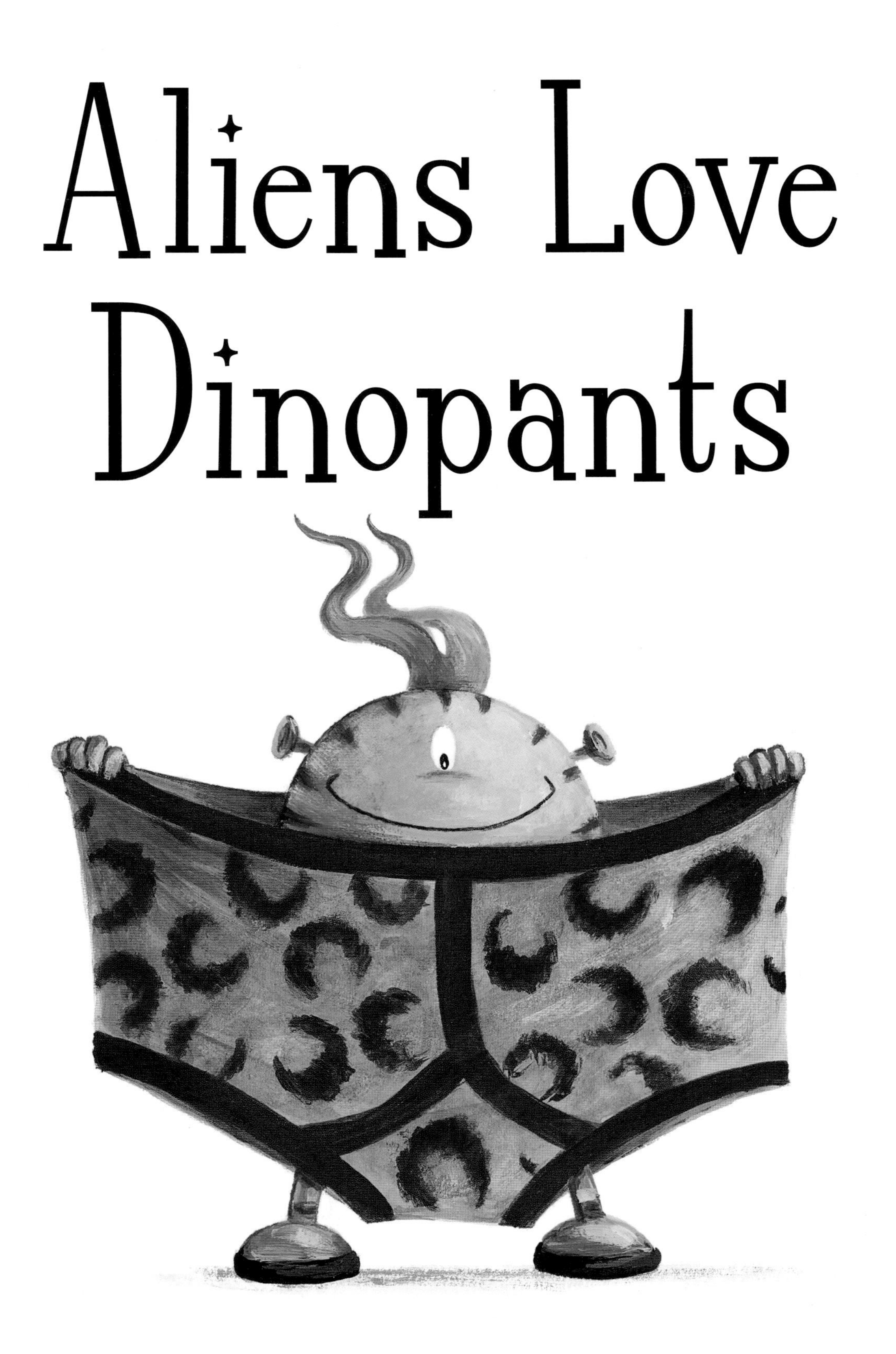

Claire Freedman & Ben Cort

SIMON AND SCHUSTER
London New York Sydney Toronto New Delhi

A band of pants-mad aliens
Zoomed down here, when SURPRISE!
Bright lightning hit their spaceship, BANG!
And hurled them from the skies.

Crash-landing in thick jungle,
"Whoops!" the aliens gasped. "Oh dear!"
But their pants-tracker was BLEEPING.
How could underpants be **here**?

The aliens trekked through tangly trees,
The signal getting stronger.
Through slimy swamps, down deep ravines,
Could they go on much longer?

Their tracker went BLEEP BONKERS!
"Wow! We must be close," they cried.
It led them to a hidden gate.
"Let's take a peep inside!"

BLEEP! BLEEP! YIPPEE!
They'd found them
(Those aliens are so clever!)
A stash of such gigantic pants,
Each pair could stretch forever!

"We'll take these pants!" the aliens laughed.
But . . . RAAAAR! They heard loud roars!
And found themselves surrounded BY . . .

GINORMOUS DINOSAURS!

The dinosaurs were furious.
"Hands off our pants!" they roared.
"We'll fight you pesky aliens,
To save our precious hoard!"

The aliens almost fainted!
"DINOSAURS? This can't be so!
You dinos were wiped out from Earth,
Pants-zillion years ago!"

"We hid down here," the dinos said.
"The humans didn't see!
We saved our pants, but daren't come out.
We wish we could roam free!"

"We ALL love pants," one alien cheered,
"So there's no need to fight!
I have a plan to get you out
And save you from your plight!"

Those busy aliens got to work,
With laser tools and saws.
They hammered, welded, chopped and drilled,
Helped by the dinosaurs.

"TA-DAH! A super dino-pod
To launch you into space!
We'll take you to our planet,
ZOOM! A most pants-tastic place!"

"Our new home's great!" the dinos said.
"There's underpants for all!"
It's fun the games that can be played
With pants both HUGE and small.

So when your washing's on the line,
Quick! Guard it at the double.
With aliens AND dinosaurs,
There's twice pants-pinching trouble!

50

50